For Omi. Big, big kiss and on to one hundred!
M.S.

For Koen and for Rabbit
M.v.H.

Text copyright © 2007 by Mathilde Stein
Illustrations copyright © 2007 by Mies van Hout
Originally published in the Netherlands by Lemniscaat b.v. Rotterdam, 2007,
under the title *De kindereter*
All rights reserved
Printed in Belgium
First U.S. edition, 2008

CIP data is available

Lemniscaat
An Imprint of Boyds Mills Press, Inc.
815 Church Street
Honesdale, Pennsylvania 18431

Mathilde Stein & Mies van Hout

The Child Cruncher

Lemniscaat

HONESDALE, PENNSYLVANIA

IT WAS SUMMERTIME.
My friends were all on vacation,
my dad was stuck in his study,
the dog just wanted to sleep, and I …
I was sooooo bored!

Then one evening, a big, hairy hand
lifted me off the ground. I was thrilled! At last,
someone to play with!

"Got you!" growled a harsh voice. "You're coming with me!"

But I said, "One moment, please. I have to ask my dad first. ... Dad! I'm being kidnapped by a big, ugly villain. Is that all right?"

"Oh, that's fine," Dad replied. "Just remember to brush your teeth. Have fun."

And off we went in a wild dash through the forest.
I'd never been on a horse before, and I nearly fell off.
Fortunately, the villain had a great long beard to hold on to.

We galloped for hours. When we finally reached the villain's den, he scowled and pushed me forward.

"Get in!"

That was fine by me. I was ready for a snack. But I couldn't find the door. I stumbled, and then the villain tripped, too. He almost tumbled to the bottom of the ravine. Well, I didn't trip him on purpose, really!

I pulled him up and said *sorry* in my most polite voice, but the villain was in a foul mood. He stomped off to bed without saying good night. *Humph.* If he was going to behave like that, I might as well have stayed at home.

I had to do something to cheer him up.
I had an idea.
Maybe if I ... while he slept ...

"Surprise!"

The villain gazed around him with big round eyes. His mouth fell open, but he didn't say a word. He was just too happy to speak. That happens to me sometimes, too.

"I'm glad you like it," I said cheerfully. "But I'm getting very hungry now. Let's have some toast and eggs for breakfast."

The villain started jumping
up and down madly and roared
lots of words I couldn't
understand.

When he leapt toward me, I finally
understood what he meant. Pirates! Great! That's
the game I love best at school. But our teacher
never allows us to make so much noise.
"Break-fast," bellowed the villain.
"Break-fast, come heeere!"

"Yes. It's about time we ate something." I pointed at the chickens and asked, "Would you like your eggs fried? Your toast crunchy?"

But the villain roared, "Eggs? Toast? Not for me! I only crunch … children!"

Well, I never! Suddenly, I lost my appetite. He wasn't a nice villain at all! I'd been looking forward to many adventures, only to end up with an ordinary old child cruncher!

He growled and waved wildly and pointed to the cooking pot. "No, thank you. I don't want to play with you. I'm going home," I said. And I ran.

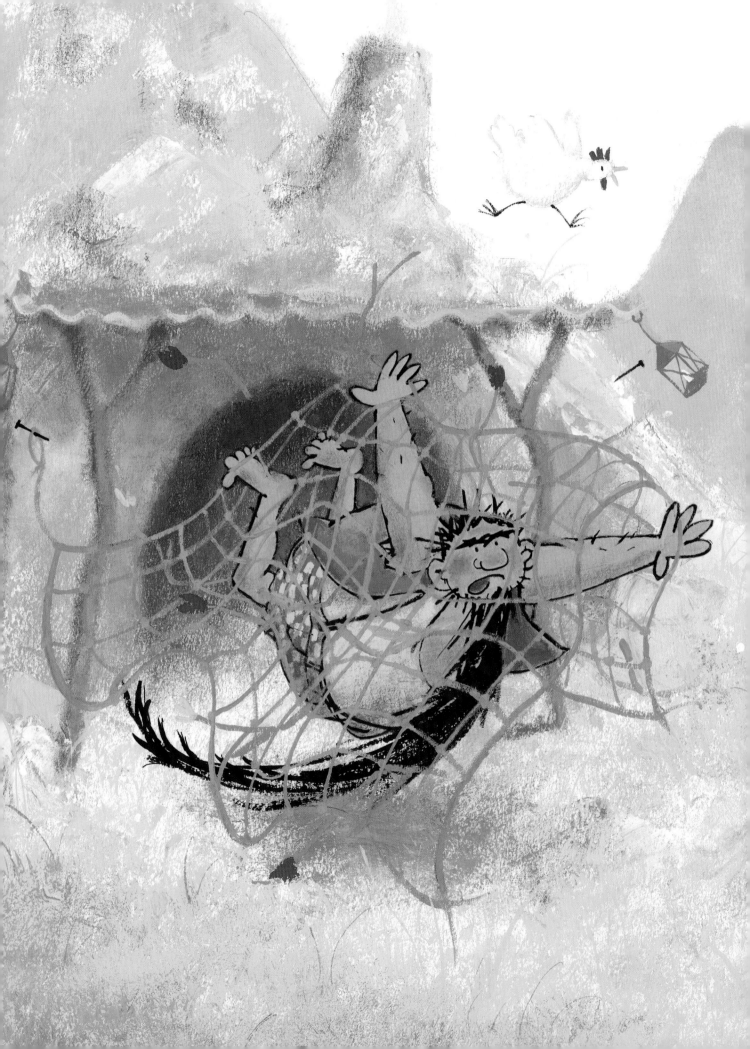

The child cruncher ran right after me. He was in such a state. "Look at you," I said, concerned. "You're all red in the face. You'd better take it easy now. Do sit down. I'm sure your horse will remember the way back to my house. There's no need for you to see me home."

But the child cruncher ran down the path right behind me until the police officer gave him a fright. Then he fell. I didn't know how to stop the horse, so I shouted, "Good-bye!" and galloped away. It was great to be sitting in the saddle this time. I could see everything!

"Hi, Dad. I'm home," I said.

"Hello, sweetie." My dad looked up absentmindedly. "You're back early. Didn't you have fun?"

"It was okay, but I forgot my toothbrush. Oh, by the way, I've borrowed the child cruncher's horse."

"Very well, dear," my dad replied. "Just put him in the garden, will you? Then get into your pajamas and choose a story. I'll come up to read to you in a moment. Nothing too frightening though, otherwise you won't sleep."

Good old Dad. Always
worrying about nothing!